JUST LIKE DAD

BY GINA AND MERCER MAYER

*For Justin and
Sara Hamaguchi*

A GOLDEN BOOK • NEW YORK

Golden Books Publishing Company, Inc., New York, New York 10106

When I grow up, I want to be just like my dad.

I'll be able to hit the baseball right out of the park, just like Dad.

Well, at least I'll be able to hit it.

I'll have a big garden, just like Dad. This is *my* garden. Maybe I'll remember to water it when I'm just like Dad.

I'll have a great job, just like Dad.
I'll have a briefcase, too. But I'll play video
games on my computer all day long.

When I grow up, I'll be able to drive a car, just like Dad.

Now he lets me sit on his lap and pretend to drive.

I'll be a great cook, just like
Dad. He cooks lots of eggs.

I'll have my own money, just like Dad.
My dad says he hopes I have a lot more.

When I grow up, I'll be able to climb a ladder to wash the windows, just like Dad.
I won't even fall.

And I'll be able to build a fence, just like Dad.
I'll know how to use a hammer and a
screwdriver and everything.

I'll be able to cut the grass with the tractor, just like Dad. He says he can't wait until I can do that.

When I grow up, I'll be able to paint the shutters, just like Dad. And I won't even get yelled at when I make a mess.

I'll be able to watch anything I want on TV, just like Dad. But I won't ever watch the news.

I'll take showers instead of baths, just like my dad. When I'm just like him, I won't want to play with my tub toys anymore. Maybe.

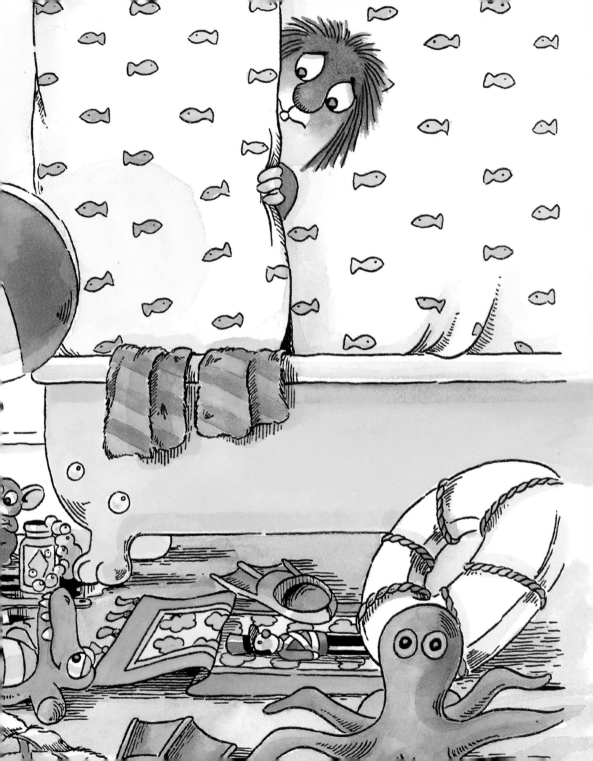

When I grow up, I'll be able to shave, just like
Dad. I'll be really careful not to get cut.

And I'll wear cologne, just like Dad. Then Mom will think I smell good, too.

I'll be able to go grocery shopping, just like Dad.
I'll buy anything I want.
I won't even have to ask.

And I'll eat a bowl of cereal every night before bed, just like Dad. Only I won't eat the kind he eats.

When I grow up, I'll be handsome, just like Dad. He's the most handsome critter in the whole world.

But most of all I'll be a great dad, just like my dad.

Then when my little critters grow up, they'll want to be just like me.